W9-CIJ-039

Caillou

At the Sugar Shack

Adaptation from the animated series: Carine Laforest
Illustrations taken from the animated series and adapted by Mario Allard

 chouette dhx media

One spring morning Caillou and his family were visiting their friend Jonas in the country. It was sugaring season, so Jonas had invited them to his sugar shack. The sun was shining, but there was still plenty of snow on the ground. Caillou liked the sound the sleigh bells made when the horses moved.

Caillou noticed a bucket hanging on a tree.

"Let's go have a look," Jonas said. He pulled on the horse's reins.

Caillou ran toward the bucket. "What's in there?"

"It looks like water, but it's sap from inside the maple tree," Mommy said. "See, it comes out through a tap."

Caillou was surprised that something that looked like water could come out of a tree. Jonas set the bucket on the ground and took out a plastic cup from his jacket pocket.
"Would you like a taste?"
He filled the cup with sap. Caillou and Rosie took turns sipping it.
"Mmmm. It's sweet," said Caillou.

"We can make all kinds of great treats from sap," Daddy said. "Things like maple syrup, maple sugar, or even yummy maple butter!"
"But first, we need to collect some sap," Jonas said.
"I want to help!" Caillou exclaimed.
Jonas showed him how to take the bucket down from the tree.

"Can you carry this bucket to the sleigh?" asked Jonas. It was hard to walk in the snow, but Caillou was careful not to spill any sap. Jonas poured the liquid into a barrel, using a filter to get rid of debris.

"Let's bring the sap back to the sugar shack and turn it into maple goodies."

Inside the sugar shack, Jonas boiled the sap until it became a beautiful golden color.

"Look at this!" Daddy exclaimed. "The sap has turned into maple syrup."

Caillou couldn't believe it. The watery maple sap had become thick and dark.

"Can I taste it?" asked Caillou.

"It's too hot right now," Jonas said. "Let's wait a bit."

"While the syrup cools down, why don't you prepare the table outside? We're going to need some snow," Jonas said. "I'll join you soon with a surprise."
"We'll get right on it," Daddy said.
Caillou and Rosie filled their buckets with snow and poured it onto the table.
"Great job!" Daddy said, spreading the snow.

When the table was ready, Jonas came out carrying the saucepan.

"Careful, it's still very hot. The more you boil the maple syrup, the thicker it gets," Jonas explained. Caillou and Rosie stood back a little.

"It smells good!" Caillou exclaimed. He couldn't wait to see what Jonas's surprise was.

Jonas used a ladle to spoon the hot liquid from the saucepan. "Why are you pouring it on the snow?" Caillou asked.

"The snow cools the syrup off," Jonas answered. "This is my favorite treat of all. It's maple toffee. Try this, partner."

Jonas gave them each a wooden stick to roll
the toffee into a lollipop.
"This is the best maple toffee I've ever tasted,"
Daddy said.
"Mmm!" Mommy agreed.
"Sticky!" added Rosie.
Caillou was having a hard time with his stick.
"Do you want some help, Caillou?" Daddy asked.
"I can do it," Caillou replied.

Caillou was determined to roll the toffee onto the stick
by himself.
But it was so slippery!

Caillou had to use two sticks to roll it into his mouth.
It was definitely worth the effort.
"Maple toffee is my new favorite treat!" Caillou said.

Text: adaptation by Carine Laforest of the animated series CAILLOU,
produced by DHX Media Inc.
All rights reserved.
Original story written by Kim Segal
Original Episode #174: The Sugar Shack
Illustrations: Mario Allard, based on the animated series CAILLOU
Coloration: Eric Lehouillier

The PBS KIDS logo is a registered mark of PBS and is used with permission.

Chouette Publishing would like to thank the Government of Canada and SODEC
for their financial support.

Books
Tax Credit

Gestion
SODEC

Bibliothèque et Archives nationales du Québec and Library and Archives
Canada cataloguing in publication

Laforest, Carine, 1967-
Caillou at the sugar shack
(Clubhouse)

For children aged 3 and up.

ISBN 978-2-89718-467-4 (softcover)

1. Caillou (Fictitious character) - Juvenile literature. 2. Sugar bush - Canada
- Juvenile literature. 3. Sugar maple - Canada - Juvenile literature. 4. Maple
syrup - Juvenile literature. I. Allard, Mario, 1969-   . II. Title. III. Series:
Clubhouse.

SB239.M3L33 2018   j633.6'45   C2017-941568-9

Printed in Canada
10 9 8 7 6 5 4 3 2 1 CHO2018 OCT2017

MIX
Paper from
responsible sources
FSC® C103304